The Garden in Our Yard

by Greg Henry Quinn
Illustrated by Lena Shiffman

SCHOLASTIC INC. Cartwheel B·O·O·K·S®

New York   Toronto   London   Auckland   Sydney

For Pam
— G.H.Q.

For Emily and Ian
and wonderful Franke
— L.S.

ISBN 0-590-48536-9

Text copyright © 1995 by Greg Henry Quinn.
Illustrations copyright © 1995 by Lena Shiffman.
All rights reserved. Published by Scholastic Inc.
CARTWHEEL BOOKS is a registered trademark of Scholastic Inc.

12 11 10 9 8 7 6 5 4 3 2 1   5 6 7 8 9/9 0/0

Printed in the U.S.A.   24

First Scholastic printing, April 1995

It's spring again.
The ground warms up
And life begins to stir.
The beetles, bugs,
And butterflies
Begin to buzz and whir.

The ground is hard.
We break it up
With shovels, rakes, and hoes.
The soil feels soft
And smells so nice
As breezes start to blow.

We dig and bend,
And push and pull,
Get dirty, tired, sore.
This work is hard,
But it feels good.
Tomorrow we'll do more.

The soil's prepared
When spring's bright sun
Warms up the mother earth.
We plant our seeds
And then wait for
The miracle of birth.

Watermelons,
Broccoli,
And pumpkins fat and round —
All these and more
Will grow up from
Our seeds beneath the ground.

The seeds lie
In the darkness.
We water from above.
Now we must wait
Until they sprout
Into the foods we love.

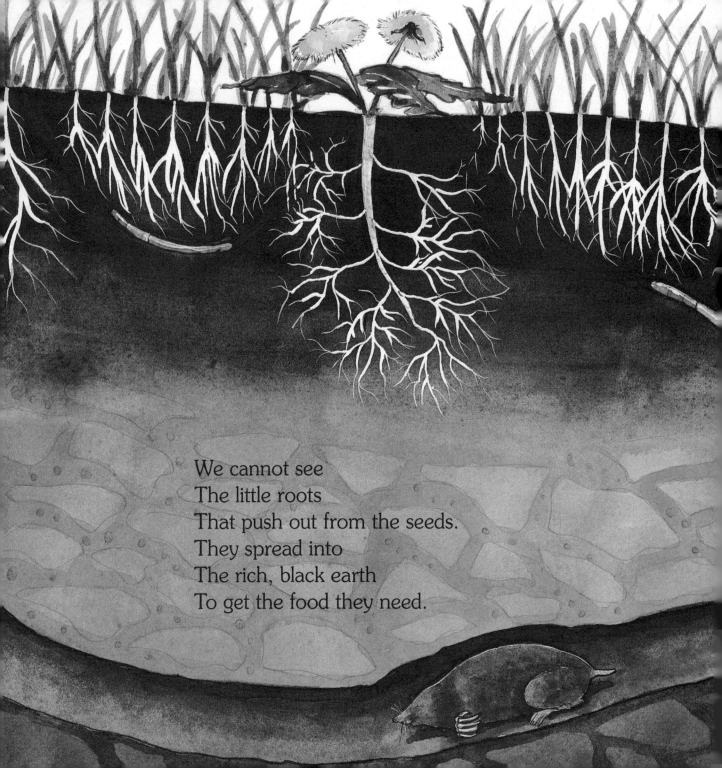

We cannot see
The little roots
That push out from the seeds.
They spread into
The rich, black earth
To get the food they need.

As robins sing
And sparrows chirp,
We see two tiny leaves
Appear above
The places where
We planted all our seeds.

The leaves unfold
To face the sun,
Which makes them turn bright green.
Up pop two more,
Then, twenty-four
Can easily be seen.

The garden's
Always changing.
We go there every day.
We pull the weeds,
And water,
And chase the bugs away.

There are lots of
Good things growing.
The waiting part is hard.
At last . . . it's time
For picking
From the garden in our yard.

We find bright
Red tomatoes,
And crooked yellow squash,
A black eggplant,
Long green beans, and
Carrots we must wash.

Spring becomes
The summertime.
And summer turns to fall.
The squirrels hide nuts
And leaves fall down.
We hear the black crows call.

The growing
Season's over.
The plants begin to die.
A cool wind tells
Tomato leaves
To wave their last good-bye.

And we feel sad
To see it end.
We loved our garden so.
But we all know
It needs to sleep
Beneath the cold, white snow.

One day we put
Our sweaters on
To walk the garden path.
We see the cold,
Hard, frozen ground,
But we begin to laugh.

For soon we know
That spring will bring
The sun and gentle rain.
And we will take
Our tools and seeds
And garden once again.